NINA AND THE TRAVELLING SPICE SHED

Also published by Tamarind Books:

Camp Gold: Running Stars

Camp Gold: Going for Gold

Skin Deep

The Young Chieftain

Spike and Ali Enson

Spike in Space

Nina and the Travelling Spice Shed

Madhvi Ramani

Illustrated by Erica-Jane Waters

Tamarind

NINA AND THE TRAVELLING SPICE SHED
A TAMARIND BOOK 978 1 848 53089 8

First Published in Great Britain by Tamarind Books,
an imprint of Random House Children's Publishers UK
A Random House Group Company

This edition published 2012

1 3 5 7 9 10 8 6 4 2

Set in Bembo MT

Tamarind Books are published by Random House Children's Publishers UK,
61–63 Uxbridge Road, London W5 5SA

www.**tamarindbooks**.co.uk
www.**totallyrandombooks**.co.uk
www.**randomhousechildrens**.co.uk

Addresses for companies within The Random House Group Limited
can be found at: www.randomhouse.co.uk/offices.htm

THE RANDOM HOUSE GROUP Limited Reg. No. 954009

A CIP catalogue record for this book is available from the British Library.

Printed and bound by CPI Group (UK) Ltd, Croydon, CR0 4YY

Chapter One

The car crawled forward a few centimetres, then stopped again. Nina wished the long line of vehicles in front would vanish. It was Monday morning and she couldn't wait to get to school.

"What are you doing at school today?" said Dad, catching Nina's eye in the rear-view mirror. Mum turned and looked at

her expectantly from the passenger seat.

"Nothing," muttered Nina, looking out of the window.

"Nothing!" cried Dad. "They hardly give you any homework and now you're not even doing anything in school! I tell you, in India . . ."

Nina rolled her eyes. Dad was always going on about India. In India the children were cleverer; in India the weather was hotter; in India parents got more respect. It drove her crazy.

"Actually, today—" she started, but instantly regretted it. She had avoided telling them all weekend.

"Today what?" asked Dad.

"Today," Nina went on reluctantly, "everyone in the class has to pick a country from a list that Miss Matthews has made. Then we have to prepare a presentation on that country for Friday. Whoever does the best one gets a mystery prize!"

“Is India on the list?” asked Mum.

“Yeah,” sighed Nina.

“We’ve got loads of books on India at home!” said Dad.

“And photos,” said Mum.

“You can show off our souvenir of the Taj Mahal!”

“And you can talk to Aunt Nishi. She lived there almost all her life.”

“She’s nutty!” said Nina, even though she loved her aunt. Her house was filled with old books and ancient artefacts – along with modern gadgets: Aunt Nishi even had the

latest PlayStation. Nina often went there when she was bored or needed cheering up. There was no denying, however, that her aunt was eccentric. She was some sort of computer whizz who worked for the government – although no one knew exactly what she did – and as Dad always said, "Genius and madness go hand in hand."

"Besides, I'm not choosing India," continued Nina.

Mum and Dad turned to look at her in disbelief. The car was crawling slowly forward again, but the van in front had stopped.

"Dad! Don't look at me – look at the road!"

Dad remembered that he was driving and managed to brake just in time.

"But India's a wonderful country to do," said Mum. "And you're Indian – it's only right."

“I’ve never even been to India,” said Nina. “Anyway, I want to do America.”

“America!” cried Dad. “How’s America better than India?”

“America’s got Disney World, Hollywood and fried chicken – all India’s got is hot weather and poor people.”

Dad turned to face Nina again. He looked genuinely hurt. Nina felt bad – she was always disappointing her parents, even though she didn’t mean to. Before Dad could say anything, there was a thud, and everyone jolted forward – they had hit the van in front.

"I've never even been to India," said Dad.
"Anyway, I want to go to America."
"America!" cried Dad. "How? America
is worse than India!"

[illegible]

and fried chicken [illegible] all India's got is the
weather and poor people."
Dad turned to look [illegible] again. He looked
[illegible]
[illegible]
[illegible]
thing, every [illegible] with them, and everyone joked
[illegible]

[illegible]

[illegible]

[illegible]

[illegible]

[illegible]

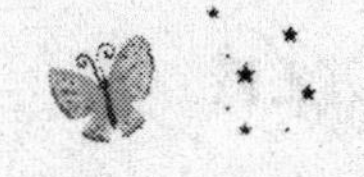

Chapter Two

By the time Dad had sorted things out with the van driver and dropped Mum off at work, Nina was late for school.

"Sorry I'm late, Miss Matthews," she said as she stumbled into the classroom. "Did I miss the chance to choose a country?"

"I'm afraid so," said Miss Matthews. "But don't worry, there's one country left, and I think it might just be the one you wanted . . ."

Nina looked at the board. The United States of America was crossed out. Brazil, China and Denmark were crossed out. In fact, everything was crossed out except . . . India! Why did everyone assume that she wanted to

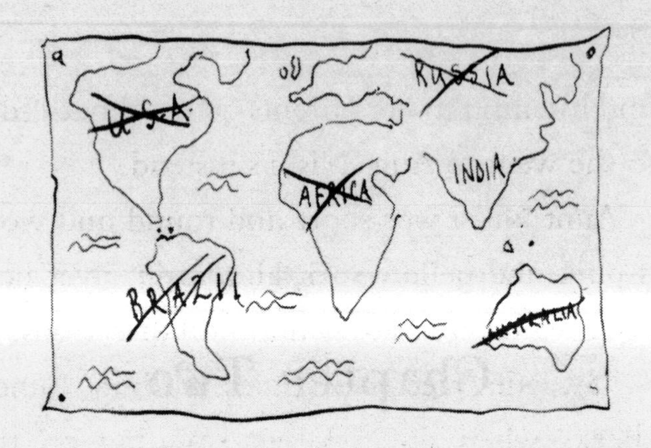

do that country? India was horrid. She had no chance of winning the prize now. She walked over to her table with a heavy feeling in her stomach, and slumped into her chair.

"We left that one for you," hissed Simon, who sat near her, "because you're from there."

No, I'm not, thought Nina. *I'm from here, like everyone else.* But she didn't say anything. Simon was the biggest bully in the class and had a habit of throwing anyone who caused him offence into the big wheelie bins at the end of the playground.

After school, she didn't feel like going home

and listening to her parents go on about India so she went to Aunt Nishi's instead.

Aunt Nishi was short and round and wore a pink and yellow sari. Her curly silver hair bounced around her head in all directions.

"Sweetie pie!" she said, pulling Nina's cheeks when she saw her standing on the doorstep.

Nina winced. "Auntie, you really have to stop treating me like a baby—" she started, but Aunt Nishi had rushed back into the house before she could even finish her sentence. Nina followed her as she shoved gadgets,

tools and papers into chests and drawers as she went. She thought she saw the words TOP SECRET stamped on one of the papers but was distracted by the smell of food. Her stomach rumbled. She had hardly touched her lunch because she was so dismayed at the thought of all the pointless research on India that lay ahead of her.

In the kitchen, Aunt Nishi threw handfuls of curry leaves and chopped tomatoes into a pot, while Milo, her robotic dog, whizzed around her feet cleaning up any bits of food she dropped by scooping them up with his metallic tongue.

"Cooking is a science," she said. "You have to do everything just so in order to get it right."

Nina watched her aunt sceptically. She did not seem to be doing things in a very scientific way.

"What are you making?" Nina hoped that it wasn't curry again. At home she nearly always had curry, whereas Aunt Nishi had a reputation for making unusual dishes.

"Something very special. I've been trying to figure out the recipe for years and now I finally I have it. I just need to add . . ." Aunt Nishi peered into her tin of spices. "Drat! I've run out of turmeric! I'll have to go to the spice shed to top up. Of course, fresh is always better, but you can only store—"

A shrill ringing noise interrupted her. It was the old-fashioned phone hanging on the wall. The type where you had to pick up the fist-sized receiver and hold it to your ear while you spoke into the mouthpiece on the main bit of the phone. Nina had never heard it ring before. She had always assumed it was a useless antique. She went to answer it.

"Oh no! You can't answer that one!"

Nina froze. Her aunt didn't usually have a problem with her answering the phone.

Aunt Nishi put her hand on the receiver and glanced sideways at Nina through her cinnamon-brown eyes. She quickly took off her gold necklace. "Here. Run down to the spice shed to fetch some turmeric," she said.

A tiny gold key dangled from the necklace.

"But—"

"All the jars are labelled. And do *not*," she said, putting on a stern face, "touch anything else."

Wow, she's a bit over-protective about her spices, thought Nina as Aunt Nishi picked up the receiver. Nina would have liked to hang about to listen to her aunt's conversation, but it was clear that she did not want her around. Besides, the emptiness in her stomach was growing and she didn't want to spoil whatever it was that Aunt Nishi was cooking, so she hung the gold chain with the key safely round her neck and slipped out of the back door.

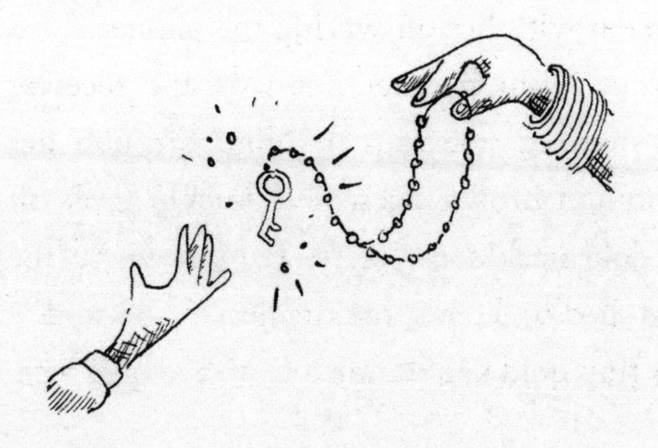

Chapter Three

Nina walked through the unkempt garden towards the shed. It was old and crooked and almost completely camouflaged by the tall grass and weeds that surrounded it.

How strange, thought Nina, looking at the gold key that hung from her neck. *I never noticed that the spice shed had such a small lock.*

Come to think of it, even though Nina had played in Aunt Nishi's garden often, she had never been inside the shed. It had always been strictly off-limits.

She leaned forward to unlock the door with the key still hanging round her neck, and decided that Aunt Nishi must have given her the wrong key after all; it didn't fit. Nina fumbled around with it a bit more to be sure. Just as she was ready to give up, there was a click, and she pushed the heavy door open.

She stepped inside. A light came on automatically as the door closed behind her. In the dim light of the single bulb that hung from the ceiling, she saw that two sides of the shed were lined with glass jars filled with different coloured spices. A heap of old junk was stacked along the back wall.

Nina's nose tingled. The air in the shed felt heavy with dust and spices, and when she looked at the light bulb, she saw thousands of

multi-coloured particles whizzing around it.

She walked slowly along the shelves reading the neatly labelled jars . . . NUTMEG, PAPRIKA, SAFFRON, TURMERIC. She picked up the large jar containing yellow powder with both hands, careful not to touch anything else. When she got to the door, she balanced the jar in one hand with the help of her knee, and attempted to open the door with the other. The tingling sensation in her nose got worse, and all of a sudden she sneezed! The jar fell and smashed. Yellow powder flew in all directions.

Nina looked at the mess in horror. Aunt Nishi seemed awfully touchy about her spices. Nina could just imagine how upset she'd be, especially since she was relying on this turmeric stuff for that special recipe she'd been attempting for years! She might even tell Mum and Dad. Nina could hear the lecture as she looked at the turmeric scattered all over the dusty floor: *In India, the children never spill turmeric, spoil a good dish, ruin their auntie's day* . . . Not even a pinch was salvagable.

She looked around for a broom. The very least she could do was clean up the mess she'd made. She searched through the junk at the far end of the shed: a Mexican sombrero, diving equipment, a pair of snow boots, an umbrella . . . What on earth did Aunt Nishi need all this stuff for? Behind it all, a broom-stick rested against the wall. She grabbed it, but to her surprise, it swung forward like a lever. Nina heard a low whining sound. She spun round.

"Wow."

A wide flatscreen TV came sliding down into the shed just behind the light bulb. It showed a detailed map of the world. Above it were the words:

TOUCH SCREEN TO GO TO DESTINATION

"I wonder what it is . . ." Nina whispered. A computer game? Or maybe something to help with her project? Her hand wavered in front of the screen, stuck between America and India. Her nose itched, and she sneezed again. Her hand accidentally brushed the screen and the shed shook, causing her to fall onto the dusty, turmeric-strewn floor.

She got to her feet again. *Stupid shed*, she thought. *Probably one of Aunt Nishi's inventions gone wrong.* She tried to dust herself down, but only ended up rubbing the powder deeper into her clothes. When she looked up, she noticed that the message on the screen had changed. It now read:

WELCOME TO MOUNT DIA, KASHMIR, INDIA

Strange. Nina went to the shed door and tried to push it open. There was something blocking it. Her heart raced as she pushed harder. Finally the door gave way, and Nina stumbled out into a pile of snow. The door shut behind her.

Chapter Four

Nina shivered. She was surrounded by mountain peaks. There wasn't a house, car or person to be seen. She stared in awe at the sparkling whiteness surrounding her. Where was she? What had happened to Aunt Nishi's garden? What if she was stuck in this winter wonderland for ever? She had to go home. She turned round to go back into the shed, but just as she did so, she glimpsed a flash of orange on the mountainside to her right. It looked like a flame dancing in the wind.

I wonder what that is? she thought. She set off towards it, hoping it would provide some clue as to what was going on.

Her feet sank into the cold, wet snow and soon began to ache. As she approached it, she saw that the speck of colour was actually a skinny, ancient man dressed in an orange cloth. His hair had grown so long that it twisted around him like a plant. His nails looked like sharpened pencils. He was sitting so still, with his legs crossed and his hands resting on his knees, that Nina thought at first he had frozen to death. Then she noticed his smoky breath.

"Excuse me," she said. No reaction. Maybe he was deaf. She stepped forward cautiously and tapped his shoulder. He didn't stir. She tapped him harder. Still he didn't move. She bent down and shouted, "HELLLLOOOOOO!" into his ear.

The man opened his eyes and frowned.

"What do you want? I'm busy!" he said.

"Um . . . It's . . . er, it's unbelievable really . . . "

"Spit it out. I'm losing my patience!"

"Well, I'm from England, and that's my aunt's shed, where she stores her spices—"

"You brought me out of forty-nine years of meditation just to tell me this?" yelled the man, his eyes becoming wide with rage. Nina backed away, a little scared. "I can tell you're from England just by looking at you," he continued, eyeing her school uniform.

"And frankly, travelling via spice shed is amateurish. I can travel to different places with the power of my mind. In fact, before you rudely brought me back, I was in Brazil, enjoying the carnival."

Brazil? Travelling via spice shed? She thought about the screen, the jolt and message that said— No, but this wasn't . . .

"Where am I?"

"India, of course – where else would you find a Mystic Sadhu like me?"

"But . . . I thought India was hot."

"Look around, girl – you think it's going to be hot in the Kashmiri mountains?"

Nina's teeth chattered and her stomach growled. She was beginning to think that this man was crazy.

"I'm not crazy!" said the man.

Nina's mouth dropped open.

"Yes, yes, I can read your thoughts. The mind is a wonderful thing! With it, you can change yourself into a coconut tree, you can bend metal without touching it, you can—"

"Can you conjure up some food?" asked Nina, thinking about the steaming pots of food bubbling away in Aunt Nishi's kitchen.

"Food? Haven't touched the stuff since 1947, but" – he dropped his voice to a whisper – "if you're hungry, I, Mystic Sadhu, can reveal to you a cosmic secret."

Nina moved closer.

"The best restaurant in the world is The Mogul, in the capital city of this great land. Go forth in your spice shed and order the potato curry – it's divine. The restaurant's near the Red Fort, on the corner – you can't miss it."

The man tore off a little piece of his orange cloth, put a handful of snow in it, and wrapped it up, muttering something under his breath all the while. He handed it to Nina.

"Take this on your travels. It will transform

into anything you wish – but don't use it for selfish purposes like getting yourself scrubbed up, or replacing some of that turmeric you spilled," he said, eyeing Nina's yellow-stained uniform, "or else you'll get bad karma."

"What's karma?"

"If you were any stupider, you'd be a fish! Karma is energy – do good things and you attract good energy, do bad things and bad things come to you. Now off with you!"

Nina shoved the parcel of snow into her pocket and turned to make her way back to the shed.

"It's hot there – perfect weather for weaklings like you!" yelled the Sadhu after her, cackling uncontrollably.

Chapter Five

The echo of the Sadhu's laughter followed Nina all the way back to the shed. Her fingers trembled with cold as she fumbled to unlock the door. It was difficult to get the tiny key into the right position to open the lock. Nina feared that she might be stranded in the Kashmiri mountains for ever! Fortunately the lock clicked and the door opened.

Inside, it seemed dark compared to the bright whiteness outside. Nina carefully stepped over the smashed glass and spilled turmeric and looked at the screen. All she had to do was touch London, and she'd be back in Aunt Nishi's back garden. She raised

her finger to the screen, then paused . . .

Maybe she ought to pick up some turmeric before going back. After all, turmeric was an Indian spice, and it would be silly to come all this way and not get any. But exactly where in India did one go to buy turmeric? Obviously not the Kashmiri mountains. The Sadhu had mentioned the capital city, and Nina's mum always went into central London whenever she wanted to do some serious shopping because she said you could get everything you wanted there. It must be the same in India.

The only problem was, she had forgotten what the capital of India was. Was it New

Delhi or Mumbai? Both were marked on the map in bold, but there was nothing to indicate which one was the capital. Nina couldn't face going out in the cold again to ask the Sadhu. She would have to guess. New Delhi . . . Mumbai . . . New Delhi . . .

Nina placed her finger on Mumbai. The shed shook once more, but this time she held onto the broomstick so she wouldn't fall. The message on the screen now read:

WELCOME TO MUMBAI, MAHARASHTRA, INDIA

She took a deep breath, pushed the door

open and stepped outside. A scooter whizzed by, dangerously close, tooting its horn. She staggered backwards. Then she heard a thudding sound and was shocked to see a bullock pulling a cart; it was galloping towards her. Nina jumped back once more, nearly hitting a car. She turned and ran in fright.

"Ouch!" She had run straight into a boy.

"Are you OK?" he asked, but Nina barely heard him. She stood on the crowded pavement gazing at Aunt Nishi's spice shed. It was positioned in the middle of a busy road, with bicycles, cars, scooters, rickshaws, buses, and even cows negotiating their way around it. If this was how they drove in India, no wonder Dad was always having accidents.

It was sweltering, so Nina took off her jumper. As she was doing so, she noticed the boy she had bumped into, waiting patiently for an answer. He was barefoot, and almost blended into the dusty street with his brown skin, faded clothes and straw-like hair.

"Oh! Yes, I'm OK, thanks," she said.

"You must have hit your head hard – it

took you ages to answer that simple question. By the way, I'm Raj."

"Nina."

"You have a funny accent. Are you an NRI?"

"What's an NRI?"

"A non-resident Indian."

"I'm not really Indian, but my parents are . . . Is this the capital?"

"You must have concussion. This is Mumbai – New Delhi's the capital. Here, have some water," said Raj, picking a bottle of water out of the bag of a lady passer-by and offering it to Nina.

Nina looked at the bottle. She wasn't sure about taking stolen goods, even though she was thirsty. A little further up the street, the woman from whom Raj had swiped the water was frantically searching through her bag. Nina took the bottle and went over to her, leaving Raj staring at the shed and scratching his head.

"People in this city are building shacks faster than you can say vegetable biriyani," he muttered to himself.

Nina held out the bottle of water. "I think this is yours."

The woman looked Nina up and down. "Street kids! I should have known. Keep the water – just give me the envelope."

"What envelope?" asked Raj, who had come to stand next to Nina.

"Don't you play clever with me! There was an envelope in my bag and now it's not there! If you took the water, you must have swiped the envelope too!"

Raj started to protest, but then a strange look came over his face. "Oh my God! It's Maya Mistry!"

"Shhh! You little urchin, don't go telling the whole world – I'll be surrounded by fans and paparazzi in no time. Just hand back my envelope, and Maya Mistry here will give you a part on my new film," said the woman.

"But we don't have it," said Raj.

The woman looked crestfallen. "If you don't have it, then . . . Oh, I dread to think . . . What am I going to do?" Tears filled her eyes and she turned to walk away.

Raj stopped her. "Don't worry, I'll find it for you!"

"But how?"

"I'll just ask around. I know most of the pickpockets and thieves around here."

The woman looked at Raj sceptically, then shrugged. "Well, I suppose it won't do any harm."

"And if—"

"Yes, yes, if you find it, you'll get a part in my film," said the woman, who now seemed to be getting short-tempered. "It's black with silver writing on it, but you'll have to get it to me within an hour. I have a busy schedule. Locate the envelope and you'll know where to find me."

With that, she spun round on her heel and disappeared into the crowd. *What a temperamental woman*, thought Nina. Her strangeness seemed to have rubbed off on Raj, who looked dizzy and was muttering to himself.

"Omigod. Maya Mistry. Must find envelope. Omigod . . ."

"Maya who?" said Nina.

"That accident must have knocked your brains out! Look," said Raj, pointing at a billboard with a beautiful woman posing on it. Although the woman in the picture was smiling and wearing a red sari and

lots of jewels, there was a striking similarity between her and the lady they had just encountered. Across the billboard were the words:

PYAR, THE HOTTEST FILM OF THE YEAR,
STARRING MAYA MISTRY

"We have to find that envelope! I've always dreamed of Bollywood!" said Raj.

Nina surveyed the jam-packed street. Finding an envelope in this city would be like searching for a needle in a haystack. "I'll help you," she said. Four eyes were surely better than two.

So off they went, keeping their eyes peeled for the envelope. Nina's shoes and socks, which had got wet in the snow, soon dried off as she and Raj walked along a curved, palm-tree-lined boulevard called Marine Drive. On one side, the breeze from the glittering ocean

refreshed them, while the sun bounced off the big bright buildings on the other. Nina had always imagined that this was what Miami in the USA would look like, not Mumbai. Raj pointed out Chowpatty Beach, where families gathered around vendors selling all sorts of snacks, but Nina and Raj couldn't afford to eat anything as they had a deadline to meet.

Whenever they stopped to talk to somebody, Nina studied the traffic and tried to figure out what rules the drivers were following. She saw a car reversing onto a roundabout, a rickshaw on the wrong side of the road, and buses, vans, cars and scooters cutting across each other whenever they felt like it, without even indicating. Raj just strolled across the roads like he owned them. He seemed to know everybody – the pickpockets, the beggars, and the people in living in little shelters made of rags, sticks and corrugated iron. Nina liked Raj, even though he wouldn't believe her story about the travelling spice shed. He insisted that she was imagining things because of the bump on her head.

As they walked, he told her the best ways to get money off rich adults. His top three tricks were: pretending that he had been hit by one of their cars, then asking for compensation; walking around wearing sunglasses and pretending to be blind; and – an oldie but a goldie – making his eyes big and wide and sitting on the pavement with a sad expression on his face.

At the Gateway of India, Raj did an impression of King George V, for whom the great structure had been built when he visited India in 1911. Maybe Raj had what it took to become a great actor after all, thought Nina.

After almost an hour of walking around in the heat and asking scores of people, they still hadn't found the envelope. Raj flopped down onto the pavement.

"There goes Bollywood," he sighed. Someone dropped a coin into his lap because he looked so forlorn. Nina sat down next to him, and felt something cold against her thigh.

She brought the bundle of snow out of her pocket. Miraculously, it hadn't melted. What had the Mystic Sadhu said? That it would change into anything you wished – but not to use it for selfish purposes. She looked at Raj. Helping him to come one step closer to his dream of becoming a star, as well as helping Maya to recover her envelope, seemed like a good cause. She closed her eyes and wished that it would transform into Maya Mistry's envelope.

When she opened her eyes, Raj was staring at her hands in awe. In place of the snow was

a black envelope with Maya Mistry's name and address written on it in silver ink.

"That's the envelope! Just like she described!" shouted Raj, jumping up and hailing a rickshaw. "Chalooo! We only have ten minutes to get to Maya's house!"

Chapter Six

Nina and Raj arrived at Maya's address just in time. The two guards standing in front of the huge golden gates saw the black envelope and let them into the magnificent front garden, bursting with exotic plants and flowers. They walked up the long path to the door of the mansion and rang the bell. A servant invited them in. Nina was thankful that the house was air-conditioned as the heat outside was becoming unbearable.

The servant led them into a big room decorated with hand-crafted oak furniture, embroidered silk curtains, intricate batiks and solid gold statues of Indian gods, where Maya paced up and down the marble floor reading a script. Raj proudly held out the envelope.

"Oh – that's it! But how . . . ? I doubted you would . . ." she said as she took the envelope from him and pressed it to her heart. She laughed and put her arms around them both.

"Just goes to show that anything is possible in Mumbai! Come on – I'm late for my shoot!"

The three of them climbed into a black limo, which weaved dangerously through the Mumbai traffic to the location of the film set.

When Nina got out of the car, she gaped at

the bright lights, huge cameras and frenzied activity going on around her. She'd hardly had time to take it all in when a fat man with grey hair came striding towards them.

"Darling, you're late!" he said to Maya. Nina reckoned that he was the film director.

"Fashionably so. I picked up some new talent on the way," she said, smiling at Nina and Raj.

"Oh, as if we didn't have enough people! Where's my first assistant? Farooz! Deal with these two!" And with that, the director took Maya by the arm and led her away.

Farooz came hurrying up to Nina and Raj. He was skinny, with small puffy eyes and a big clipboard overflowing with notes. He eyed Nina's turmeric-splattered uniform.

"Getting into character already, I see," he said. Nina had no idea what he was talking about. "Right, the next scene shows the town celebrating Holi. You know what to do."

He ushered them onto a set where lots of different people were milling about. All around were big gold plates heaped with different-coloured powders.

Holi? Why did that sound familiar? Nina turned to Raj, but before she could ask him, the director's voice boomed through the megaphone.

"Lights! Camera! Action!"

Raj grabbed a fistful of pink powder and threw it at Nina! She looked around. Everyone was running about throwing coloured powder at each other. Of course! The word "Holi"

sounded familiar because Nina's mother had described it to her. It was a festival of colour that she had celebrated as a child in India! Nina grabbed some purple powder and chased Raj. They laughed and squealed as coloured powder went flying through the air.

"Cut!"

Everyone stopped. Nina looked around at the mess, trying to catch her breath, and was reminded of the turmeric scattered all over the shed. Aunt Nishi would be worried, and Nina still hadn't got any turmeric! She turned to Raj.

"I need some turmeric – and some help to get back to that shed."

Raj saw the desperate look on Nina's face. "I can get you back to the shed, but I have no idea what turmeric is."

They quickly said goodbye to Maya, who was getting her hair done. She invited them back onto the set tomorrow. Just before they left, Nina made one last attempt to locate some turmeric.

"Maya, do you know where I can get some turmeric powder?"

"Oh, sweetie. My servants do all that. Besides, I never allow that powder stuff into my house. I only use fresh. Turmeric flowers are my favourite. I always keep some in my dressing room – see?" she said, showing Nina a beautiful white flower.

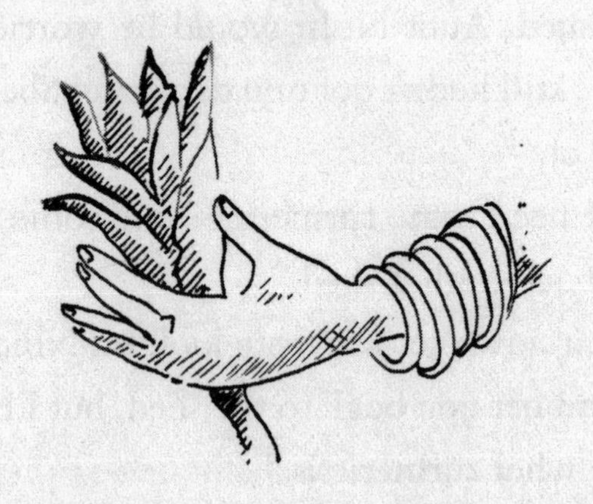

"The turmeric grows underneath, where the roots are," she continued.

Nina nodded, thinking how unfortunate it

was that the three people she had met in India – a Mystic Sadhu who hadn't eaten since 1947, a street boy, and a rich actress – had no idea about something as simple as getting hold of a common Indian spice.

"Where are you going in your travelling shed now?" Raj asked with a cynical smile as he led Nina smoothly through the traffic to the shed in the middle of the road.

"I have to return to England," said Nina.

"I know you said you're from there, but you know, you have a lot in common with us Indians: you're kind and generous and fun and . . ."

"What?"

"A little bit mad!"

Nina laughed. "Well, goodbye then," she said sadly. She had grown quite fond of Raj.

"Thanks for your help with the envelope. I wish I could give you something in return . . ."

said Raj, searching his pockets. He smiled and pulled out a little bottle. "Here – take this Jackal Jell. Us thieves pour it into locks on doors and windows to open them. I suppose I won't be needing it any more since I've got some paid work now."

Nina put the bottle into her pocket, unable to work out what good it could possibly be to her.

Raj made a silly face at Nina. "Still, there's as much chance of that shed going anywhere than there is of me being the next big Bollywood star . . ."

Chapter Seven

The door shut on Raj and the noisy Mumbai street, and Nina looked at the screen. She was about to touch home when she noticed a big area on the map labelled NATIONAL PARK. She remembered Maya Mistry's words: *I only use fresh* . . . Maybe she ought to go and see if she could find some fresh turmeric there; after all, it would only take a second. She would step out, have a quick look around, and come straight back. Nina touched the screen; the shed shook, and the message read:

WELCOME TO SUNDERBANS NATIONAL PARK,

WEST BENGAL, INDIA

The first thing that struck Nina when she opened the door was the vibrant sound of birds. A green and blue parrot swooped past the doorway. Nina stepped out and looked around. A river flowed nearby, and on the river bank was a cluster of white flowers, exactly like the one Maya Mistry had shown her!

Nina went over and plunged her fingers into the wet soil. She dug up one of the flowers and saw the thick orange roots underneath. Finally! She had it. She put the whole flower, root and all, into her pocket and stood up.

She looked at the river flowing before her. Everything seemed so peaceful. In fact, even the birds had stopped chirping. She caught sight of something in the water. It looked like an animal swimming in the river – but what was it?

The creature was getting closer. Nina thought it looked like a cat – which was impossible because everyone knew that cats hated water. Besides, it looked a bit too big to be— Nina gasped. The animal was metres away from her now, and she realized that it was a tiger! She turned and ran back towards the shed.

She was almost there when she slipped and fell in the mud. Aunt Nishi's necklace went flying from around her neck. The tiger rose up out of the water. The glint of the gold key in the sunlight caught its eye. It prowled towards Nina with narrowed eyes.

Nina jumped up, grabbed the key and

frantically tried to open the door with it, but it was no good. She was in a state of panic, and her hands were shaking with fright. She wasn't sure if her fear was making her imagine things, but she was sure she could feel the tiger's warm breath on her back.

The Jackal Jell! thought Nina, taking the bottle out of her pocket. She poured it into the keyhole, opened the door, and dived into the shed as the tiger pounced.

The door closed just in time, and Nina almost fainted with fear as she heard the tiger's paws thud against it. The shed rattled as it clawed at the wood. Nina scrambled over to the screen – the shed was rickety enough already and she was sure it wouldn't withstand the tiger's furious strength for long – and jabbed London.

Chapter Eight

All was silent. *Wow*, thought Nina. India was . . . surprising. She jumped when she heard a frantic banging at the door. Then she heard Aunt Nishi's voice. She opened the door and hugged her aunt.

"Where on earth have you been?" cried Aunt Nishi. "I came out to see what was taking you so long, saw that the shed was gone and assumed the worst! Kidnapped by the gangs in Mexico, eaten by a cheetah in the Serengeti, swallowed by an erupting volcano in Iceland, surrounded by yodellers in an Austrian village . . ."

"It's OK, Aunt Nishi," said Nina, taking

the white flower out of her pocket. "I was just fetching some turmeric!"

Even though Aunt Nishi took the fresh turmeric from Nina, and used it to finish her cooking, she was not amused. In fact, she was so angry that her hair looked more frazzled than ever! Over dinner, she insisted that Nina relate everything she had been up to for the past two hours. By the time Nina had finished her story, Aunt Nishi had relaxed a little, and her hair was almost back to its old bouncy self.

"Mmmmm – that was the most scrumptious curry I've ever had!" said Nina, trying to get

back into Aunt Nishi's good books.

"I got the recipe off the owner of The Mogul in New Delhi," said Aunt Nishi, smiling.

Now it was Nina's turn to ask the questions. "Aunt Nishi, did you invent the travelling shed? How does it work? What do you use it for?"

"Yes, I invented the shed, with the help of a few physicist friends of mine. We used the principles of quantum physics—"

"Quantum what?"

"You're too young to understand exactly how the shed works. You're too young to know about it, and you are especially too young to use it! But since you *do* know about it, you must promise to keep it a secret."

Aunt Nishi looked more serious than Nina had ever seen her before. Nina agreed to keep the shed a secret, but she wished that her aunt would tell her more.

"But why?" she asked. "You could make a

lot of money if you offered people rides in it."

"The shed is not a form of entertainment. If the wrong people used it, it could cause problems. Maybe one day, when you're older, I'll tell you more about it – but now we really must get going. I phoned your parents to tell them that you were staying for dinner, but they'll be expecting you back. Oh, and I'll be needing that key, please."

Nina reluctantly handed the chain with the tiny gold key over to Aunt Nishi. There were so many other places she wanted to visit!

When Aunt Nishi dropped Nina home that evening, her parents took one look at her muddy, multi-coloured uniform, and demanded to know what she had been up to. Although Nina wanted to tell them the truth, she kept her promise to Aunt Nishi, and told them that her uniform had got dirty while she was playing with her friends.

Besides, they probably wouldn't have believed her anyway.

"Children here!" yelled Dad. "They don't know the value of things! I tell you, in India . . ."

Chapter Nine

For the rest of the week Nina stayed out of trouble and worked hard on her presentation. She looked at the books, photos and souvenirs that her parents gave her. She went to the library, researched on the Internet, and talked to Aunt Nishi. Mum and Dad were pleasantly surprised by her new-found interest in India.

On Friday morning Nina nervously fidgeted in the car on the way to school.

"I tell you, in India," said Dad, "the children don't study half as hard as you have. You'll do well."

Nina smiled, and felt a bit more confident.

However, by the time it was her turn to get up in front of Miss Matthews and the entire class, she was nervous again. She talked about the capital, New Delhi, the Bengal tigers, who had adapted to their environment and were good swimmers, and Bollywood, the Indian film industry, which produced even more films than Hollywood.

As she talked, she started to relax. She told everyone about festivals such as Holi, and the Mystic Sadhus who meditated in the mountains of Kashmir, and passed round a miniature model of the Taj Mahal and samples of Indian spices that she had borrowed from Aunt Nishi. She had even talked her mum into making some samosas for the class.

"Mmm, these are yummy," said Simon, stuffing his face with more than his fair share.

After everybody had finished their

presentations, they had a short break while Miss Matthews made her decision. Everybody talked excitedly about who they thought would win, and what the mystery prize might be.

"I bet it's a boring encyclopaedia," said Simon.

"I bet it's something fun, like tickets to a musical," said Sara, who loved anything to do with dancing and singing.

"I bet it's a sports car!" said Jimmy, forgetting that he couldn't drive.

After the break, Miss Matthews got up to announce the winner.

"I've had a most educational afternoon. All the presentations have been wonderful and you all put a lot of effort into them. However, only one person can win the mystery prize . . ."

Nina crossed her fingers and prayed that it would be her.

"And that person is Nina! She found out so much about her country, and her vivid presentation really transported us all to the magical, diverse land of India."

Nina couldn't believe it. Everybody clapped as she went up to the front of the class. Miss Matthews presented her with a red envelope, and she ripped it open. Inside was a card that read:

You have won a meal for you and your family at any of the following restaurants:

Curry and Spice
Frankie's French Bistro
Mangia Italiano
Taste of China
The All-American Diner
The Swedish Meatball Factory

When Nina got home and told her parents, they were ecstatic.

"Oh, I've been wanting to try out that Indian restaurant for ages," said Mum.

"But," said Nina, "I want to go to the All-American Diner."

Mum and Dad were silent for a moment. "Well, since you've worked so hard, you deserve to go wherever you choose," said Dad. "And I do love fried chicken!"

"Yes," said Mum. "We're so proud of you."

Later that evening, Nina watched a programme on the latest Bollywood news with her parents. She didn't like Bollywood films, but now she had a reason to check what was going on in the industry – she wanted to keep an eye on Raj's career! On the television, the presenter announced that they had some exclusive clips of the new Maya Mistry film.

A colourful Holi scene appeared on the television.

Nina saw herself on screen and was just about to say something, but she stopped herself just in time.

"Hey, that little girl looks incredibly like you, Nina," said Dad.

"It's a shame she'll never be able to experience Holi like we did," said her mum.

"She's even wearing a—"

The bell rang. It was Aunt Nishi, which was a surprise because she hardly ever stepped out of her house.

"Sweetie!" she said, pulling Nina's cheeks. She dropped her voice to a whisper. "Your parents told me about your success at school. I'm glad that your little voyage in the shed helped. After all, you know what Euripides said: 'Experience, travel – these are an education in themselves.'"

Nina nodded, even though she had no idea

who Euripides was. "Does that mean I can use it again, Aunt Nishi?" she said.

"We'll see," said Aunt Nishi with a twinkle in her eye.

About the Author

Madhvi Ramani was born in London, where she studied English and then Creative Writing at university. Like Nina, she enjoys having adventures in different countries. She also likes blueberries, dark chocolate and books. She lives in Berlin with her husband and imaginary cat. You can follow her on Twitter @MadhviRamani

Where would you like Nina to travel next? If you have a suggestion, please send a letter to Madhvi Ramani, c/o Tamarind, 61–63 Uxbridge Road, London W5 5SA

Nina's Fantastic Facts about India

Want to learn more about Karma? Well, if you play Snakes and Ladders, you can! This fun board game was invented in India and shows how Karma works. The ladders represent good deeds, which send you higher up the board, and the snakes represent bad deeds, which send you back down.

In Mumbai, 1,000 films are produced every year and over 14 million cinema tickets are sold in India every day – that's a lot!

The Taj Mahal was built in 22 years and it took more than 1,000 elephants to help build it!

In India, turmeric powder is often used on cuts, as it's known to help heal wounds.

Aunt Nishi's Yummy Potato Curry

Serves 4

Ingredients:

Oil
1 tsp cumin seeds
4 curry leaves
1 cinnamon stick
1 onion, finely chopped
1 tsp grated garlic
1 tsp grated ginger
1 red + 1 green chilli
(if you like it hot!), finely chopped
1 teaspoon salt

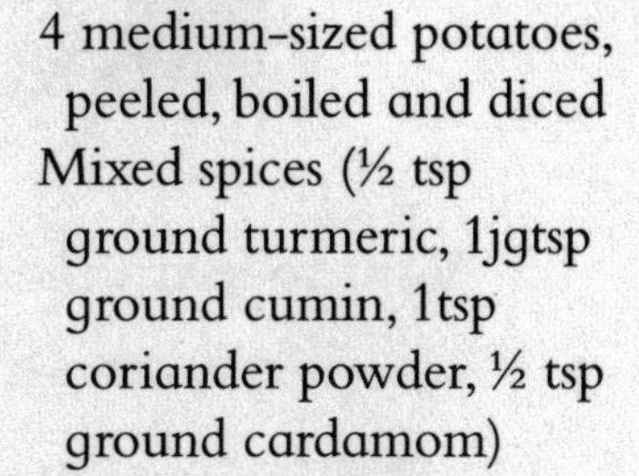

4 medium-sized potatoes, peeled, boiled and diced
Mixed spices (½ tsp ground turmeric, 1jgtsp ground cumin, 1tsp coriander powder, ½ tsp ground cardamom)
2 tbsp tomato puree
Water
½ cup yoghurt, beaten
Handful of fresh mint

What to do

(make sure you have a grown-up to help you!)

1. Heat the oil in a pan. Add cumin seeds, curry leaves and the cinnamon stick.
2. When cumin seeds turn a darker brown, add onion, garlic, ginger and chillies.
3. Sprinkle on half the salt and fry the onions.
4. Add potatoes, stir, then sprinkle on the mixed spices and remaining salt. Stir for 2 minutes.
5. Add the tomato puree and enough water to just cover the potatoes. Simmer on a low heat for 5 minutes.
6. Pour in the beaten yoghurt and stir for 2 minutes.
7. Add mint leaves. Serve with rice or naan bread.

Coming soon:

Book 2

NINA AND THE KUNG FU ADVENTURE

See yourself in our books